W9-CPM-940

RICHARD SCARRY'S
The Supermarket Mystery

How is food mysteriously disappearing from Grocer Dog's supermarket? Ace detectives Sam and Dudley shadow suspects to crack the case and catch the criminals.

RICHARD SCARRY'S
The Supermarket Mystery

STERLING CHILDREN'S BOOKS
New York

Sam Cat and Dudley Pig are very fine detectives.
If anyone has a problem, they will try to solve it.
Grocer Dog telephoned to tell them that he had a problem.

Sam and Dudley drove to Grocer Dog's supermarket to see if they could solve it.

Dudley parked the car outside the supermarket.
My! Where did Dudley ever learn how to drive?

Grocer Dog told Sam and Dudley that someone had been stealing food from his supermarket.

The only way out was through the checkout counter. Someone had been sneaking food out of the store without paying for it.

"It's a mystery to me how they do it," said Grocer Dog.

"Then we will find out," said Dudley.
"But first we must put on our disguises.
We don't want the robber to know who we are."

Sam and Dudley went into Grocer Dog's private office. Dudley always keeps disguises in his umbrella. Whenever he and Sam want to look like someone else, they put on costumes from Dudley's umbrella.

Just look at that nice lady shopper coming out of Grocer Dog's office!
And what is that in her shopping cart? Why, it is a sack of potatoes!

You wouldn't know that was Sam and Dudley, would you? Now, don't tell anyone!

"Keep your eyes and ears open," Dudley said to Sam Potatoes.
"The robber is probably stealing food this very minute."

"Cootchie coo," said Dudley.
"What a cute little baby bunny! But you are much too thin.
Your mother should feed you more to fatten you up."
"That's not a baby bunny, Dudley," said Sam Potatoes.
"It's a bunny doll."

A few minutes later Dudley said,
"SAM! I have solved the mystery!
I know how the robber steals! Look!
There she is now!"

This is what Dudley saw. Can you tell which one is the thief? Are you sure?

Dudley rushed across the supermarket.
He grabbed a lady's hat off her head and
smashed it to the floor.

"I've got you now!" he shouted.
"That's not make-believe fruit on your hat.
It's REAL fruit and you were going to steal it!"

"Just you look!" said the lady.
"You have ruined my new hat!
You think you're so smart!
Here! You just eat one
of these REAL apples!"

Dudley took a bite of the apple.
It was not a real apple.
It was made of cloth.
And it was stuffed with feathers!

Poor Dudley!

Dudley was sorry that he had ruined the lady's hat. To show everyone that he was really a nice lady, he helped Mother Bunny pick out a watermelon that she couldn't reach.

"Now please try to catch this one," said Dudley.

Meanwhile Sam Potatoes was keeping his eyes and ears open.

"Dudley," said Sam.
"Did you notice how FAT that bunny doll is getting?"

Dudley was not paying too much attention to what Sam was saying.

"Sam, look!" he shouted. "There's the robber! This time I'm sure of it!"

Dudley ran off through the store.

A lady shopper wished to buy a sack of potatoes. Sam Potatoes escaped from her just in time.

"That lady crocodile is the robber!" said Dudley. "She is hiding stolen food in her baby carriage."

Dudley smashed into the baby carriage.
But there was no stolen food inside it.
Mother Crocodile was furious!

"Just when I finally get my darling little babies to sleep,
you have to come along and awaken them!" she said.
"Dudley! Dudley! I could have told you she wasn't the thief!"
said Sam Potatoes. "I know who is doing the stealing!"

For once Dudley paid attention.
"Who is it?" he asked. "How do you know?"

"There is no time to explain now," said Sam.
"The robber has to leave by way of the checkout
counter. Hurry there! It's that lady with . . .

"... the FAT-"

Before Sam could finish talking —**Sploshhh!**

Klonk!

Dudley landed in a pickle barrel!
Sam landed on his head.
Sam was knocked unconscious!

"How dare you call ME fat?" said the lady.
"And where did you ever learn how to drive?"

But look! Someone is picking up a sack of potatoes!

Suddenly Dudley noticed that Sam was missing.

"Sam knows who the robber is. I must find him," said Dudley.
He asked the fat lady, "Where is my sack of potatoes?"

"A bunny lady took it to the checkout counter," she said.

Dudley rushed there, but the bunny lady didn't have Sam Potatoes.
Mother Bunny was saying to Grocer Dog, "I have decided not to buy
any food today, after all."

Grocer Dog replied, "That's what you say every day, Madam."

Dudley took a closer look and wondered,
"But how does she feed her baby bunny?"

Then suddenly he remembered what Sam had said earlier:
"That's not a baby bunny. It's a bunny doll."

And my! That doll had grown very, very FAT!

"STOP THIEF!" cried Dudley as he leaped out of his disguise. "Your bunny doll is stuffed with stolen groceries!"

Mother Bunny was the thief!

BUT NO! It was not a mother bunny at all!
The thief was Blackfinger Wolf,
the wicked supermarket robber!
He had been wearing a bunny disguise.
He threw his bunny mask away.

Out of the supermarket the robber fled.
Dudley didn't have time to look for Sam.

He had to catch Blackfinger Wolf all by himself.

Hurry, Dudley!

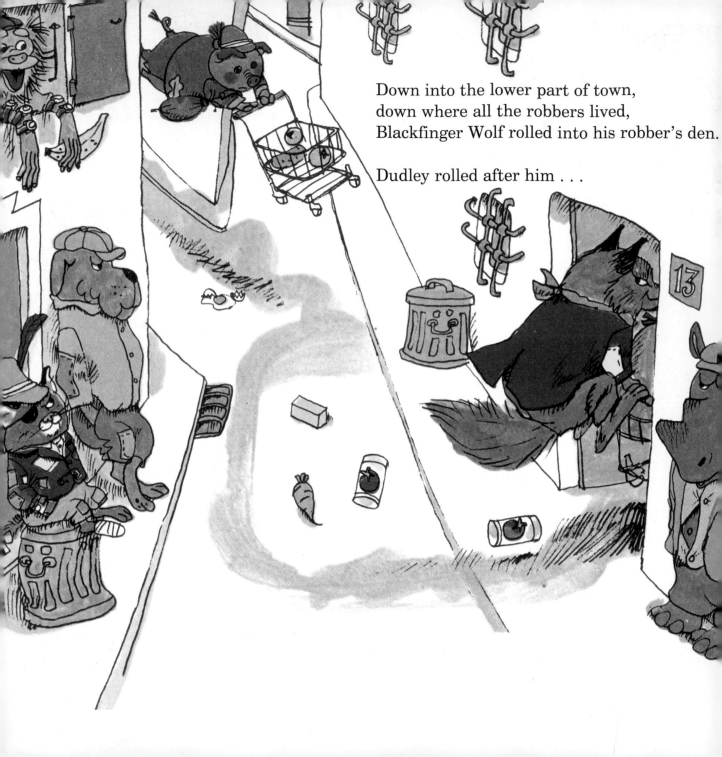

Down into the lower part of town,
down where all the robbers lived,
Blackfinger Wolf rolled into his robber's den.

Dudley rolled after him . . .

... right into a trap!

Poor Dudley!
"Oh! I wish Sam was here," he moaned.

Just then the doll began to move and walk.
"HELP!" screamed Blackfinger.
"The doll is alive!

HELP! SAVE ME!"

Blackfinger let go of the rope and started to run away.

Crrrump!

Dudley landed on top of him.
But Dudley was afraid of the doll, too!
"HELP! SAVE ME!" he shouted.

The doll stopped in front of him.

Zzzip!

Out of the doll stepped a sack of potatoes.
And out of the sack of potatoes stepped Sam!

"SAM! It's you!" said Dudley happily.
"DUDLEY! It's you!" said Sam. "But how did I get here?"

Then Dudley explained. "Your disguise was so good that Blackfinger Wolf thought you were really a sack of potatoes. When you were knocked unconscious, he stole you, too!"
"He was a very clever thief," said Sam.
"But we are very clever detectives, aren't we?"
Dudley grinned.

STERLING CHILDREN'S BOOKS
New York

An Imprint of Sterling Publishing
387 Park Avenue South
New York, NY 10016

Published in 2014 by Sterling Publishing Company, Inc.
in association with JB Communications, Inc.
41 River Terrace, New York, New York
Previously published in 2008 by Sterling Publishing Company, Inc., in one volume with two other Richard Scarry titles (*The Great Pie Robbery* and *The Great Steamboat Mystery*) under the title *The Great Pie Robbery and Other Mysteries* (hardcover)

ISBN 978-1-4549-1011-4

Distributed in Canada by Sterling Publishing
c/o Canadian Manda Group, 165 Dufferin Street
Toronto, Ontario, Canada M6K 3H6
Distributed in the United Kingdom by GMC Distribution Services
Castle Place, 166 High Street, Lewes, East Sussex, England BN7 1XU
Distributed in Australia by Capricorn Link (Australia) Pty. Ltd.
P.O. Box 704, Windsor, NSW 2756, Australia

For information about custom editions, special sales, and premium and corporate purchases, please contact Sterling Special Sales at 800-805-5489 or specialsales@sterlingpublishing.com.

Printed in China
Lot #:
2 4 6 8 10 9 7 5 3 1
11/13

www.sterlingpublishing.com/kids